WHEN VALUES FADE, FORESTS FALL

How humanity's inner crisis is destroying the natural world.

@LOCAL_INITIATIVES

"Buy the book, get a unique code, and stand a chance to win ₹10,00,000!"

JAY SRI

AF517468

BlueRose ONE.com
Stories Matter
NewDelhi • London

BLUEROSE PUBLISHERS
India | U.K.

For permissions requests or inquiries regarding this publication, please contact:

BLUEROSE PUBLISHERS
www.BlueRoseONE.com
info@bluerosepublishers.com
+91 8882 898 898
+4407342408967

ISBN: 978-93-7310-326-6

Cover design: Aman Sharma
Typesetting: Manisha Rawat

First Edition: November 2025

Author Bio – JAY SRI

JAY SRI is a passionate writer, spiritual seeker, and advocate for conscious living. With a deep-rooted belief in the transformative power of ancient wisdom, her work bridges timeless philosophy with the needs of today's modern world.

She draws inspiration from the Bhagavad Gita, Indian scriptures, and real-world human experiences to guide readers toward inner peace, ethical awareness, and sustainable living. She is also the founder of B UNIQUE SENSE, a spiritual initiative dedicated to reviving traditional practices through modern formats—such as the Bhagavad Gita Writing Program.

Whether writing about human values, nature, or self-realization, her voice remains sincere, reflective, and grounded. Through her books, she invites students, professionals, and seekers alike to reconnect with truth (Satya), purpose (Dharma), and the beauty of living mindfully—in harmony with both self and nature.

She currently resides in Andhra Pradesh, India, where she continues her mission to inspire individuals to live with discipline, compassion, cultural pride, and a deep sense of purpose.

Preface

A Whisper from the Past, A Cry for the Future — JAY SRI

A Childhood Question That Changed Everything

As a child, I used to ask my mother questions that still echo in my heart:

"Mom… why was everything so beautiful back then?

When food tasted pure and soulful, and the air was fresh...

The garden felt like heaven, and the sky looked magical.

I can't forget the joy of dancing in the rain, the innocence of our games,

And how people smiled with kindness — not suspicion.

But now… everything seems to be vanishing."

"Why doesn't the food taste the same, Mom?

Why do we feel unsafe when we step outside?

Why do we hesitate before speaking to someone?"

What went wrong, Ma?

Is nature to be blamed — or are we?

With calm wisdom, she simply said:

"We must change along with time, my dear."

One evening, I asked her again:

"Ma… do you think the world will ever return to what it was?"

She smiled softly and replied:

"If time can change everything... maybe, with time, we too can change everything back."

That answer stayed with me.

Because deep **WITHIN** me,

I still believe the sun is rising.

And if the sun is still rising — there's still hope.

But I thought deeply and said:

"Mom… time hasn't changed.

The sun still rises every day without fail.

The moon still glows with grace.

Seasons still arrive on schedule.

Birds still sing.

And animals still live with discipline.

If time is flowing the same way,

Then what's truly changing… in us — humans.

We are the ones hurting nature in the name of comfort.

We chase luxury and forget the basics.

We spend hours in gyms, yet have no time to **plant a single tree**.

We spend thousands on shopping, yet forget to give a **drop of water** to a plant."

This book is dedicated to that lost innocence,

To the child who still questions…

To every heart that remembers the fragrance of soil after rain,

And to a future where nature and humanity walk hand in hand again.

It's not just about saving the Earth--It's about saving ourselves.

Contents

Chapter 1:
HUMAN VALUES AND NATURE LOSS

1.1 The Interconnection Between Human Values And Nature Loss

"When we lose our connection to nature, we lose a part of ourselves."

Long before modern civilizations rose with concrete walls and digital screens, human beings lived in harmony with nature. Trees were not just plants—they were sacred. Rivers weren't just water—they were life-givers. The sun, the moon, the wind—everything in nature was seen as an extension of the divine, and human life revolved around this deep-rooted reverence.

But this wasn't just spirituality—it was a reflection of values: **respect, gratitude, humility, empathy, and balance.**

Today, as we race forward with technological progress and urban lifestyles, the very values that once guided our relationship with the Earth are fading. And as those values decline, so too does our connection with nature.

Nature Reflects Our Inner World

Human values are the inner compass that shapes our choices, relationships, and worldview. Nature, on the other hand, is the outer world we interact with. The two are not separate—they are mirrors of each other.

- When **greed** overcomes contentment, forests are cut down for profit.
- When **ego** silences **humility,** rivers are polluted without remorse.
- When **selfishness** replaces compassion, we consume without care for what we leave behind.

In this way, the environmental crisis is not just about climate or pollution—it's a **crisis of values.**

From "I" to "We"

Human values are fundamentally about moving from **individualism to interconnectedness.** Nature operates on interdependence—every tree, insect, animal, and drop of water plays its role in balance. Likewise, human values like **empathy, service,** and **respect for all life** invite us to live not just for ourselves, but for the collective well-being.

This is why ancient traditions—from tribal wisdom to Vedic philosophy—emphasized **oneness with nature.** The Earth wasn't seen as a resource, but as a mother. This wasn't poetic—it was practical, sustainable, and wise.

A Broken Link, A Fading World

As we drift further from nature, our inner lives are also affected:

- Stress, anxiety, loneliness, and dissatisfaction are rising.
- Mental health issues are more common in cities than in nature-rich villages.
- The more we consume, the emptier we feel.

This is not a coincidence. When we disconnect from the natural world, we disconnect from the rhythm of life itself.

Reflection

If the Earth is a mirror, what does it say about who we've become?

And more importantly, who do we want to be?

1.2 Why Are We Losing Both?

"Progress without purpose leads to destruction."

In our pursuit of development, we've gained speed, but lost direction. The 21st century is marked by monumental achievements—skyscrapers, satellites, smart devices—but somewhere along this journey, we've left behind the very values and natural harmony that sustained life for thousands of years.

So the question arises—**why are we losing both human values and nature at the same time?**

1. The Race for Material Success

Modern society equates success with accumulation—more money, more gadgets, more status.

But in this race:

- **Gratitude** is replaced with **greed**
- **Contentment** with **comparison**
- **Simplicity** with **showmanship**

This shift in values fuels **overconsumption,** which in turn pressures industries to extract more resources, often at the cost of forests, rivers, air, and soil.

2. Disconnection from Roots

Traditional lifestyles were closely tied to nature—farming, seasonal cycles, and spiritual festivals celebrating rivers, trees, and animals.

Now:

- Children grow up **knowing brands more than birds.**
- Cities replace **trees with towers.**
- Celebrations mean **firecrackers and waste,** rather than gratitude to nature.

This disconnection breaks the emotional and cultural link that once taught us to protect the planet and live with purpose.

3. Technology Without Mindfulness

Technology is powerful, but without mindful usage, it becomes a tool for distraction, isolation, and excess.

- Social media glorifies **self-image,** not **self-awareness**
- Instant gratification weakens **patience** and **resilience**
- Virtual life replaces **real human bonds** and **natural experiences**

As we go deeper into screens, we move further away from nature and authentic values.

4. Lack of Value-Based Education

Education today is focused on information, not transformation.

Children are taught how to solve equations, but not how to solve conflicts.

We learn about economic growth, but not about emotional intelligence or environmental balance.

When values are not taught, they fade. And when they fade, the consequences reflect in our behavior—and in our surroundings.

5. Spiritual Emptiness

Spirituality once gave meaning, balance, and responsibility.

Without it, many feel lost, chasing success but never finding peace.

This inner vacuum leads to outer destruction—**what we lack within, we try to fill by consuming more from outside.**

Conclusion

The loss of human values and nature is not a coincidence—they are **deeply interconnected symptoms** of a world that has forgotten its essence.

To restore one, we must restore the other.

And for that, we must first pause and ask—**what truly matters?**

1.3 The Urgency of Restoring Balance

"If not now, then when? If not us, then who?"

The signs are all around us—rising temperatures, melting glaciers, vanishing forests, polluted air, and restless minds. Nature is not just sending signals—it is crying out. And alongside this, humanity is facing an invisible crisis: rising depression, broken families, moral confusion, and emotional emptiness.

The balance we once enjoyed between **inner values** and the **outer environment** has tipped. If we don't act now, we risk reaching a point **where restoration becomes impossible.**

Nature Doesn't Need Us — We Need Nature

It's important to realize that nature will survive—with or without us.

Species will evolve, forests may regrow over centuries, and Earth will find a new rhythm.

But **human life**, as we know it, depends on a fragile balance of air, water, climate, and social harmony.

By harming nature, we are cutting the every branch we sit on.

By ignoring values, we are creating a society without direction.

The Ticking Clock

Scientists warn that the next **10 to 20 years** are critical to reversing climate damage.

At the same time, **cultural thinkers and psychologists** warn that we are on the edge of a **value breakdown**—where generations grow up with no sense of community, empathy, or gratitude.

This is not just about saving trees or teaching kindness—it's about **preserving the every conditions that make life meaningful and livable.**

Change Is Possible—and Powerful

The good news is that **small efforts can lead to massive transformation:**

- A single tree can give oxygen to 10 people a day
- A single act of kindness can restore someone's faith in humanity
- A conscious household can reduce waste, save energy, and influence neighbors
- A school that teaches values can change the future of hundreds of children

We don't need perfection. We need **awareness, intention,** and **collective action.**

Conclusion: A Call to Conscience

Restoring balance isn't just a mission—**it's a moral and spiritual responsibility.**

Every moment we delay, the gap grows wider.

But every moment we act with awareness, the healing begins.

Let's not wait for a crisis to awaken us.

Let this be the moment we choose to **balance growth with goodness, power with purpose, and development with values.**

Chapter 2:
The Evolution of Human Values & Nature

2.1 Ancient Civilizations and Their Respect for Nature

"Nature was not a resource; it was a relative."

Long before industrial revolutions and digital screens, ancient civilizations lived by a profound truth—nature and human life were inseparable. The sun was worshipped, rivers were considered goddesses, trees were protectors, and animals were seen as companions in the cycle of life.

This wasn't superstition; it was spiritual ecology—a way of life that honored the rhythm of nature and placed values at the heart of every action.

Indus Valley Civilization – Living with the Land

The people of the Indus Valley built cities around rivers, practiced water conservation, and followed structured waste management—**thousands of years ago**.

Their architecture blended with the environment, not against it. They lived not to conquer nature, but to coexist with it.

Vedic Traditions – Sacredness in the Ordinary

In Indian Vedic culture, every element of nature had a divine essence:

- **Akasa (Sky/Space)** was the realm of sound and vastness
- **Agni (Fire)** was the purifier

- **Vayu (Air)** was the breath of life
- **Jala (Water)** was the nurturer
- **Prithvi (Earth)** was the mother

Daily life was infused with **rituals of gratitude** towards these elements—like offering water to the sun at sunrise (Surya Arghya), walking barefoot on the earth (Bhoomi Namaskara), meditating under the open sky to connect with higher conciousness, or planting trees during festivals.

Respect for elders, service to others, and gratitude for the earth were deeply instilled human values—not lessons in books, but ways of living.

Native American & Indigenous Wisdom

Across continents, the pattern was the same. Native American tribes, Aboriginal Australians, African tribal communities—**all saw the Earth not as property, but as a partner**. They took only what they needed, gave back when they could, and lived with deep respect for all living beings.

This reverence came from understanding one truth:

Harming the Earth is harming ourselves.

The Silent Message

These civilizations weren't perfect, but they had one thing we are losing today—a value system deeply rooted in nature's wisdom.

Their progress was measured not in profits or possessions, but in harmony and balance.

Why It Matters Today

As we stand in an age of climate crisis and moral confusion, looking back is not nostalgia—**it's necessary**.

If we can **relearn the respect our ancestors had for nature and values**, we might still shape a future that is sustainable—not just environmentally, but emotionally and ethically.

2.2 Industrialization & The Shift in Priorities

"Progress isn't always forward when values are left behind."

The **Industrial Revolution** brought unmatched progress—but at a cost we're still paying today. With machines came speed, with factories came production, and with mass consumption came disconnection—from nature, and from ourselves.

What began as a pursuit of efficiency slowly evolved into a mindset of **exploitation**—where nature became a **resource**, not a **relationship**.

From Coexistence to Control

Before industrialization, humans adapted to nature's rhythm. But with the advent of machines, steam engines, and coal-fueled power, we shifted from **coexistence to control.**

- Forests were cleared to build cities.
- Rivers were dammed to fuel industries.
- Animals became commodities.
- And human values? They quietly slipped to the background.

Productivity took precedence over compassion. Time became money. Relationships became transactions.

The Rise of Mechanized Thinking

Machines don't feel, and gradually, people too began to function like machines—valuing **speed over stillness, results over relationships**, and **profit over purpose**.

In schools, education shifted from moral teachings to job-focused learning.

In homes, storytelling around firewood was replaced by newspapers and later, television.

In workplaces, teamwork was replaced by competition.

This era didn't just transform economies—it transformed **the human heart.**

The Birth of Consumer Culture

As industries grew, so did advertising. People were no longer satisfied with what they had; they were taught to **want more**.

- More clothes.
- More food.
- More gadgets.
- More success.

Need was replaced by greed. And **greed doesn't stop**—it devours not only nature, but the values that once guided our choices.

The Value Shift

What was once a culture of **gratitude, simplicity, and community** turned into one of **individualism, accumulation, and convenience**.

We stopped asking:

"Is it right?" and began asking:

"Is it profitable?"

A Turning Point in History

Industrialization was not the villain—it gave us many comforts and advancements. But the real tragedy was **forgetting the balance** between progress and preservation.

When we **chose development over dharma**, we didn't just damage the planet—we wounded the soul of humanity.

2.3 Modern Lifestyles: Convenience Over Conscience

"We built smarter homes, but forgot to build better humans."

In today's fast-paced, tech-driven world, convenience rules our choices. From instant food to one-click shopping, from ride-hailing apps to AI assistants—**life has never been easier**.

But with this ease came an invisible cost: the erosion of our conscience.

We began to **choose what's easy, not what's right**.

Comfort Became the New God

Modern society glorifies comfort:

- **Microwave meals** over mindful cooking
- **Plastic packaging** over sustainable alternatives
- **Disposable culture** over durability
- **Scrolling** over soul-searching

We are no longer patient nor present. We consume faster than we think, and discard faster than we feel.

This comfort-first mindset has made us forget the **interconnected impact** of our choices—on the environment, on others, and on our inner values.

The Rise of "Me First" Living

In the name of progress, we adopted lifestyles that focus heavily on **self-centered success:**

- Big cars over clean air
- Trendy gadgets over ecological impact
- Career growth over community bonding
- Virtual followers over real friendships

E**mpathy, responsibility, and mindfulness** have taken a backseat to **speed, status, and self-image.**

Time-Saving or Value-Draining?

We invented machines to save time but ended up with **less time for what truly matters:**

- Family meals have become rare.
- Conversations are interrupted by notifications.
- Celebrations are for Instagram, not for intimacy.

This disconnection from others has also deepened our disconnection from **nature** and **values**.

The Silent Crisis

Our modern comforts have not made us happier—they've made us **more anxious, lonely, and disconnected**.

We lost the habit of asking:

"What is the impact of my lifestyle?"

And we stopped listening to the **inner voice** that once guided us toward empathy and ethics.

Can We Change?

Yes—but it begins by slowing down. By shifting from impulse to intention.

By choosing quality over quantity, presence over performance, and values over vanity.

The journey back to a conscious life starts with small, consistent decisions—because **modern life doesn't have to mean mindless life.**

Chapter 3:
The Silent Erosion of Human Values

3.1 Selfishness Over Selflessness: A Changing Mindset

"In chasing personal gain, we forgot collective good."

Once upon a time, our societies were built on **selflessness**—helping neighbors, caring for elders, sharing food, and standing together during difficult times. Acts of kindness weren't rare—they were **routine**.

But in today's world, this selfless mindset is slowly being replaced by **individualism and self-centered goals**.

From "We" to "Me"

Modern culture celebrates **personal success**—often at the cost of community well-being.

- People are encouraged to "look out for number one."
- Competition is seen as more important than collaboration.

- The idea of "giving back" is seen as optional, not essential.

This shift has created a society where **self-interest often outweighs shared values.**

Subtle Forms of Selfishness

Selfishness today doesn't always appear as arrogance or greed—it shows up silently:

- Ignoring someone who needs help because **"we're busy"**.
- Hoarding resources **"just in case"** while others struggle.
- Thinking, **"It's not my problem"** when we see injustice.
- Prioritizing personal comfort over social or **environmental responsibility.**

We've normalized these attitudes, calling them "practical" or "realistic," forgetting that they slowly **erode the very values that hold us together.**

The Cost of Isolation

A self-centered world isn't just less kind—it's **more lonely.**

- Relationships become transactional.
- Friendships feel shallow.
- Trust becomes rare.
- And inner fulfillment fades.

The **more we isolate,** the more disconnected we feel—not just from others, but from our own sense of purpose.

The Way Forward

True happiness doesn't come from what we take—but from what **we give.**

- Helping someone without expecting anything in return.
- Listening with full attention.
- Being kind, even when it's inconvenient.
- Making choices that benefit not just ourselves but others too.

These small acts of selflessness don't weaken us—they **strengthen our humanity.**

A Question to Reflect On

Are we raising a generation that cares—or one that only **competes**?

If we want a better world, we must begin by **bringing back the beauty of selflessness,** one act at a time.

3.2 Empathy Decline: Social Media vs. Real Connections

"We are more connected than ever, yet more disconnected than ever before."

Empathy—the ability to feel what others feel—is the glue that holds humanity together. But in a world dominated by screens, likes, and endless scrolls, **empathy is quietly fading.**

The Illusion of Connection

Social media gives the illusion of closeness:

- A birthday wish through a story

- A heart emoji on a sad post
- A "How are you?" in the comments

These gestures **look like empathy**—but often lack the **depth and presence** that real connection requires.

We've started **replacing conversations with comments,** and **support with symbols.**

The Rise of Emotional Numbness

With endless exposure to tragic news, disasters, and suffering, people feel overwhelmed.

To protect ourselves, we **emotionally disconnect.**

- "Another flood? That's sad… scroll."
- "Someone lost a loved one? Oh… next post."

This overload causes **compassion fatigue**—where we feel too drained to care deeply.

The Ego-Centered Online World

Social media encourages a **performance-based culture**:

- Curated happiness
- Filtered perfection
- Validation through likes

In such a space, t**here's little room for vulnerability**, and even less space to truly understand what others are going through.

Empathy suffers when people **compete for attention** rather than offer it.

Real Presence Is Missing

We may chat all day, but how often do we sit down and truly listen?

- No devices.
- No multitasking.
- Just one human holding space for another.

That's where **real empathy lives**—not in flashy gestures, but in silent presence.

Reclaiming Empathy in a Digital Age

Technology isn't the enemy. But our **habits** need reflection.

- Call instead of texting when someone's hurting.
- Make time for face-to-face moments.
- Pay attention, not just a reaction.
- Feel with, not just for.

When we put **humanity before algorithm**, empathy begins to grow again.

A Thought to Ponder

Are we building a world where we **understand each other**, or one where we just **observe each other**?

The more we choose **real connection over virtual validation**, the more we restore empathy—not just in others, but in ourselves.

3.3 The Vanishing Concept of Gratitude & Contentment

"In chasing what we don't have, we forget to cherish what we do."

Gratitude and contentment were once the heartbeats of a peaceful life. People felt thankful for simple joys—food on the table, a roof over their head, the presence of loved ones. But today, these values are slowly fading, replaced by **restlessness, comparison, and desire for more.**

The Endless Hunger for "Next"

Modern life teaches us: "What you have is not enough."

- Got a good phone? A better one just launched.
- Got a job? Now you need a promotion.
- Bought a car? Time to aim for luxury.

This **never-ending race** has blurred the line between **need and greed**. And in the process, we forget to pause and say: "I am truly grateful."

Comparison: The Gratitude Killer

Social media plays a big role in the erosion of contentment.

- Someone's vacation looks better than yours.
- Their family seems happier.
- Their success story makes you question your own.

We're not unhappy because we lack something; we're unhappy because someone else seems to have more.

This constant comparison **blocks gratitude**, replacing peace with pressure.

Why Gratitude Matters

Gratitude is not just a nice feeling—it's **transformative**:

- It shifts focus from lack to abundance.
- It increases happiness and reduces stress.
- It strengthens relationships.
- It helps us connect with nature, people, and even our inner selves.

Contentment is the result of gratitude—**not settling for less, but being at peace with enough.**

The Forgotten Joy of Simplicity

There's a quiet joy in:

- Watching a sunset.
- Sharing a meal.
- Helping a stranger.
- Sitting in silence with someone you love.

But in today's noisy world, simplicity is often ignored. And with it, we lose our natural ability to be **grateful and satisfied**.

Bringing Gratitude Back

It starts with awareness and small steps:

- Keep a gratitude journal: Write 3 things you're thankful for every day.

- Compliment people genuinely.
- Say “thank you” with presence—not just as a habit.
- Appreciate nature, food, time, and breath.

The more we practice gratitude, the more we see: **what we have is already a blessing.**

A Reflection

When was the last time you felt **truly content,** without needing anything more?

Gratitude turns what we have into **enough**.

Contentment turns that enough into **peace**.

3.4 Family Bonds and Community Spirit: Are They Fading?

“When homes become silent, the heart of society stops beating.”

There was a time when families were close-knit, and communities were like extended families. **Meals were shared, emotions were expressed, and lives were interwoven**. But today, those strong bonds seem to be loosening. **What happened to togetherness?**

The Rise of Nuclear Living

As urbanization grew, so did the shift from **joint families to nuclear families,** and now—more often—to **individual living.**

- Grandparents live alone.
- Children grow up without knowing cousins or neighbors.

- Busy parents hardly speak to each other.

Convenience has replaced connection, and independence has taken priority over interdependence.

Technology: Bridge or Barrier?

Ironically, we can video call someone across the world—but struggle to **talk to someone in the next room**.

- Family dinners are interrupted by phones.
- Real conversations are replaced by forwarded messages.
- Online friendships flourish while real-life bonds fade.

We are "connected" digitally, yet **disconnected emotionally**.

Community Spirit: A Dying Flame?

Communities once looked out for each other:

- Neighbors celebrated festivals together.
- Streets felt like homes.
- If someone was in need, help came before asking.

But now, in many places:

- People don't know their neighbors' names.
- Safety is doubted.
- Individualism dominates over unity.

This **loss of community spirit** creates isolation and weakens the social fabric.

The Impact of Broken Bonds

When family and community ties weaken:

- **Mental health issues** increase.
- **Children grow without emotional grounding.**
- **Elders feel abandoned.**
- **Social values erode.**

A lonely society becomes more **fragile**, vulnerable to fear, division, and mistrust.

Rekindling the Flame

It's not too late to restore what we're losing:

- **Eat together** without devices.
- **Celebrate traditions** and festivals with family.
- **Visit elders**, not just call.
- **Create community events**, even small ones.
- Teach children to **value relationships** over possessions.

Togetherness doesn't happen by chance—it happens by choice.

A Thought to Reflect On

Are we raising walls or building bridges?

Are we leaving a world where **love lives in hearts—or only in memories?**

To restore human values, we must begin **inside the home and outside the doorstep.**

Chapter 4:-
The Invisible Damage to Nature

4.1 Overexploitation of Resources: Short-Term Gains, Long-Term Loss

"We did not inherit the Earth from our ancestors—we borrowed it from our children."

Nature has always provided. From the air we breathe to the water we drink, the soil that grows our food to the trees that offer shelter—everything we need has been freely given. But in the rush for progress, we've forgotten one essential truth: **resources are not infinite.**

The Greed Behind Growth

Overexploitation happens when we take **more than what nature can regenerate.**

- **Forests** are cut down faster than they grow back.

- **Groundwater** is pumped out faster than it refills.
- **Minerals and fuels** are extracted without long-term vision.

Why? Because short-term profits and convenience often **blind us to future consequences.**

Agriculture: From Sustainable to Strained

Traditional farming respected seasons and soil cycles. But now:

- **Chemical fertilizers** and **pesticides** exhaust the land.
- **Monoculture farming** (growing one crop repeatedly) weakens soil health.
- **Overgrazing** and **deforestation** destroy biodiversity.

We're pushing nature beyond its limits—and that strain **comes back to us** in the form of poor food quality and ecosystem collapse.

Water: Abundance to Scarcity

Freshwater is becoming a luxury:

- Rivers are drying up due to overuse and pollution.
- Groundwater tables are falling alarmingly.
- Industrial waste and sewage choke natural water bodies.

We're using clean water as if it's unlimited—forgetting that only **1% of Earth's water** is available for human use.

Mining and Fossil Fuels: Earth's Bleeding Wounds

Mining leaves scars—both physical and environmental:

- Forests are cleared.

- Toxic waste seeps into soil and water.
- Fossil fuel burning increases **air pollution** and **global warming.**

While industries profit, **future generations inherit the damage.**

Who Suffers First?

The **poor and rural communities** are often the first to suffer:

- Farmers face droughts and failed crops.
- Indigenous tribes lose their forests and homes.
- Urban slums face water shortages and health issues.

The burden of overexploitation falls **unequally**, deepening **social and environmental injustice.**

Time to Rethink Our Relationship with Nature

It's not just about using less—it's about using **wisely**.

- **Sustainable resource management**
- **Eco-friendly farming**
- **Rainwater harvesting and water conservation**
- **Renewable energy over fossil fuels**

The future depends on how quickly we shift from **greed to need**—from exploitation to **regeneration**.

A Final Thought

The Earth is speaking—through droughts, floods, and wildfires.

The question is: **Are we still listening?**

4.2 Consumerism: The Addiction That's Destroying the Planet

"We buy things we don't need, with money we don't have, to impress people we don't know."

Modern life is filled with **choices and temptations**. New gadgets, new clothes, fast food, fast delivery—**everything is one click away**. But this convenience comes at a heavy cost, not just to our wallets, but to **the planet**.

What is Consumerism?

Consumerism is the **belief that happiness comes from owning more**.

- It feeds on advertising that says, "You're not enough until you buy this."
- It encourages **constant upgrades**—even if the current item still works.
- It turns people from **citizens into consumers**.

This endless craving creates a cycle of **buy-use-throw-buy again**.

The Real Cost of "More"

Every product we buy comes from the Earth:

- **Clothes** require water, cotton, dyes, and labor.
- **Electronics** need rare minerals, energy, and often exploit cheap labor.
- **Packaging** leads to mountains of plastic waste.

The planet is paying the price for our **unsustainable desires.**

Fast Fashion: Style at Nature's Expense

A single cotton shirt can use over **2,700 liters of water**—enough for one person to drink for two years.

Fast fashion promotes:

- Cheap clothes that don't last
- Mass production with poor working conditions
- Massive textile waste in landfills

We wear it once. The Earth wears the damage forever.

E-Waste: Our Growing Garbage Pile

Phones, TVs, laptops—discarded quickly for newer versions.

- Over **50 million tonnes** of e-waste are generated globally every year.
- Most are dumped or burned, releasing **toxic chemicals** into the soil and air.
- Only a small fraction is recycled properly.

We are drowning in our own convenience.

The Illusion of Happiness

Consumerism creates a **temporary high**, not lasting joy.

- People feel pressure to keep up.
- Debt increases.
- Mental health suffers due to comparison and material stress.

In chasing more, we're losing contentment and peace.

Breaking the Addiction

The solution isn't to stop consuming—but to **consume mindfully.**

Ask: Do I really need this?

Choose **quality over quantity**.

Support **sustainable brands** and **local products.**

Repair, reuse, and recycle.

Minimalism is not about less—it's about making space for what truly matters.

A Final Reflection

What we consume today, the planet has to process tomorrow.

Let's choose a lifestyle that celebrates **needs, not wants—purpose, not possession.**

4.3 Urbanization vs. Natural Ecosystems

"Cities are expanding, but at what cost? As concrete rises, green disappears."

The world is rapidly urbanizing. Cities are growing taller, wider, and denser. Roads are laid, buildings rise, and shopping malls flourish—but in the process, **forests are cleared, rivers are choked, and wildlife is pushed to the edge.**

Urbanization, while essential for development, has become a double-edged sword—**offering comfort while costing nature.**

What Is Urbanization?

Urbanization is the movement of people from rural to urban areas, often driven by the promise of better jobs, education, and lifestyle.

But this expansion demands space. And that space often comes at the cost of:

- **Forests and wetlands**
- **Fertile farmland**
- **Natural water bodies and biodiversity zones**

Vanishing Green Spaces

Natural ecosystems are self-sustaining. They regulate climate, purify air, recharge groundwater, and support life. But when trees are replaced by towers, and soil by cement:

- **Rainwater can't seep in—flooding increases**
- **Air becomes polluted—respiratory diseases rise**
- **Birds, insects, and animals lose their habitats**

We are replacing nature's balance with human imbalance.

Heat Islands and Climate Stress

Urban areas are **hotter** than rural surroundings—a phenomenon called the **urban heat island** effect.

- Roads and buildings **absorb and trap heat**
- Lack of trees reduces natural cooling
- Excessive energy use adds to the problem

As a result, cities become **hotter, drier, and more uncomfortable**, increasing energy demands for cooling—and thus contributing further to global warming.

Disrupted Wildlife Corridors

Urban sprawl cuts across **natural migration routes** and **animal habitats:**

- Animals are forced into human areas, leading to conflict.
- Roadkills, deforestation, and isolation push species toward extinction.
- Invasive plant species spread in disturbed urban areas, displacing native ones.

We're not just building homes—we're **destroying countless others.**

Water Crisis in Urban Areas

With nature gone:

- Lakes and rivers are filled up to make room for buildings.
- Groundwater levels deplete due to overuse and poor recharge.
- Rainwater drains away instead of nourishing the soil.

Ironically, cities face **water scarcity** even with advanced infrastructure.

Is Sustainable Urban Living Possible?

Yes. Urbanization doesn't have to be destructive. We can build smarter, not just bigger.

- **Green buildings** with energy efficiency
- **Urban forests and rooftop gardens**

- **Rainwater harvesting systems**
- **Eco-friendly transport and city planning**

By embracing **eco-urbanism**, we can h**armonize development with nature**.

A Final Thought

In the race to build more cities, let's not forget:

We're part of a larger ecosystem, not separate from it.

A city without nature may rise in size, but fall in **soul**.

4.4 Climate Change & Disasters: Nature's Warning Signs

"The Earth is speaking through storms, droughts, and rising seas. Are we listening?"

Nature has always been powerful—but now, it's becoming unpredictable. **Heatwaves in winter, floods in deserts, cyclones in new regions**—these aren't just random events. They are warning signs, showing us the consequences of how we treat the Earth.

Climate change is no longer a distant threat. It is **here, now, and escalating.**

What is Climate Change?

Climate change refers to **long-term shifts in temperatures and weather patterns,** mainly caused by **human activities**—especially the burning of fossil fuels like coal, oil, and gas.

These actions release **greenhouse gases (GHGs)** like carbon dioxide and methane, which trap heat in the atmosphere, leading to:

- **Global warming**
- **Unstable weather**
- **Melting glaciers and rising sea levels**

Nature's Warnings Are Loud and Clear

Every natural disaster is not just a tragedy—it is a **message**:

- **Heatwaves** are killing crops, wildlife, and humans alike.
- **Floods** are washing away homes, despite no rain in previous years.
- **Droughts** are lasting longer, turning fertile lands into deserts.
- **Forest fires** are more frequent and intense, burning entire ecosystems.

These are not coincidences. They are **reactions to human carelessness.**

The Ripple Effect of Disasters

Climate disasters don't just affect the environment—they hit **human values and societies:**

- **Food and water** scarcity causes migration and conflict.
- **Loss of homes and livelihoods** leads to trauma and depression.
- **Inequality widens**—the poorest suffer the most.
- Communities that once lived in balance with nature are being displaced and destroyed.

Climate change deepens both **ecological and emotional wounds.**

We Are Fueling Our Own Suffering

Our addiction to:

- **Cars over cycles**
- **ACs over shade trees**
- **Fast life over mindful living**

...is pushing the planet beyond its limits. And in return, the planet is **pushing back**.

The Hope: It's Not Too Late

The same hands that caused the damage can also heal.

- Reduce carbon footprints
- Support renewable energy
- Conserve forests and oceans
- Adapt sustainable lifestyles

Climate change can be slowed. Disasters can be minimized. But only if we **act together and act now**.

A Final Message

Nature doesn't need saving—we do.

Every cyclone, every drought, every heatwave is Earth's way of saying:

"Change your ways before I change everything."

Chapter 5:
Case Studies: Lessons From the World

5.1 The Amazon Rainforest: Greed vs. Green

"The lungs of the Earth are gasping for breath."

The Amazon Rainforest, often called the **lungs of the planet,** spans across nine countries in South America and produces nearly **20% of the world's oxygen.** It is home to **millions of species,** countless indigenous tribes, and a delicate ecosystem that has thrived for centuries.

But today, this green paradise is under threat—not by natural decay, but by **human greed.**

The Heart of Biodiversity

The Amazon is one of the most biodiverse regions on Earth:

- Over **390 billion trees**
- Thousands of animal and plant species found nowhere else

- Rivers that flow like arteries through its dense green body

It’s not just a forest—it’s a **living, breathing system** that maintains the global climate.

What’s Happening to the Amazon?

Every minute, **an area equivalent to a football field is destroyed.**

Why?

- Illegal logging for timber
- Forest fires—often man-made—to clear land for agriculture
- Mining and oil extraction
- Expanding cattle ranches and soybean farms

What’s being sacrificed? Clean air, fresh water, and climate stability.

The Impact: Local and Global

The destruction of the Amazon doesn’t just affect Brazil or its neighbors. It affects **all of humanity:**

- **Increased carbon in the atmosphere:** Fewer trees means less CO_2 absorption
- **Disrupted rainfall patterns:** Affecting agriculture across continents
- **Species extinction:** Losing unique lifeforms forever
- **Displacement of indigenous communities:** Along with their ancestral wisdom

The forest is **burning,** and with it, a part of our future.

The Fight to Save It

There are rays of hope:

- Indigenous tribes resisting exploitation
- NGOs and climate activists raising global awareness
- International pressure on governments for conservation
- Technological tracking of deforestation using satellites

Yet, the fight is far from over. **Economic greed often drowns out ecological need.**

What Can We Learn?

- **Greed unchecked can destroy even the richest ecosystems**
- **Modern development must never forget ancient balance**
- **Protecting forests is not charity—it's survival**

The Amazon's story is a **mirror**—reflecting what we value more: **Profit or the Planet.**

5.2 The Ganges River: From Sacred to Polluted

"What was once worshipped now weeps."

The **Ganges River,** or Ganga, is not just a river—it's a **goddess,** a **mother,** and a **spiritual lifeline** for millions in India. For centuries, it has symbolized purity, devotion, and eternal flow. People travel hundreds of miles to bathe in its waters, believing it cleanses sins and heals the soul.

But today, the sacred Ganga is burdened with **waste, chemicals, and neglect.**

The Sacred Source of Life

The Ganga stretches over **2,500 kilometers,** nourishing more than **400 million people.** Along its banks lie ancient cities like Varanasi, Haridwar, and Prayagraj—centers of culture, pilgrimage, and history.

- **Religious ceremonies,** cremations, and festivals revolve around the river.
- It irrigates farmlands that feed millions
- It is home to unique biodiversity like the endangered **Ganges river dolphin**

Yet, the river's blessings are turning into burdens.

How Did a Sacred River Become Polluted?

Centuries of reverence couldn't protect the Ganga from modern exploitation:

- **Industrial waste** dumped directly into the river.
- **Sewage and untreated water** from hundreds of cities.
- **Plastic and ritual waste** from religious practices.
- **Cremations on the banks,** leaving remains and ashes in the water.

The same hands that fold in prayer often discard waste without pause.

Consequences Beyond the Surface

The pollution of the Ganga is not just a visual scar—it's a **health and ecological crisis:**

Waterborne diseases affecting thousands annually

Decline of aquatic life, especially native fish and dolphins

Polluted farmlands due to toxic irrigation

Cultural disillusionment, as faith collides with reality

What happens when the sacred becomes unsafe?

The Cleansing Efforts

In recent years, there have been serious attempts to restore the Ganga's purity:

- **Namami Gange Mission:** A large-scale government initiative
- **Wastewater treatment plants** and stricter regulations
- **Citizen-led clean-up campaigns** and eco-awareness drives
- **Spiritual leaders** encouraging eco-conscious rituals

But reversing centuries of damage requires more than infrastructure—it needs inner transformation.

Lessons from the Ganga

- **Spiritual reverence must be matched with environmental responsibility**
- **Traditions must evolve to protect what they worship**
- **Cleansing the river starts with cleansing our habits**

The Ganga doesn't just flow through the land—it flows through the heart of India. Saving it means saving a part of the **human soul.**

5.3 Japan's Coexistence with Nature: A Model for the World

"When nature is honoured, it becomes a partner—not a problem."

Japan, a nation known for its **technological advancement,** has also maintained a deep-rooted respect for **nature and tradition.** In a world where progress often comes at the cost of the environment, Japan offers a powerful alternative: **coexistence.**

From its ancient **Shinto beliefs** to its modern **green cities,** Japan teaches that living with nature is not just possible—it's essential.

A Culture of Harmony

Nature is not separate from life in Japan—it is **woven into the soul of society:**

- Shintoism views forests, rivers, and mountains as **sacred spirits (kami).**
- Traditional architecture includes **zen gardens, wood, and open space.**
- Seasonal festivals honor **cherry blossoms, harvests, and nature's rhythms.**

In Japan, a **walk through a forest is a spiritual experience,** not just recreation.

Modern Progress, Ancient Wisdom

Even with urbanization, Japan has made deliberate efforts to **blend development with ecology:**

- **Bullet trains** coexist with **protected forests.**

- **Compact urban design** reduces land use and pollution.
- **Strict recycling laws** and **waste sorting** are part of daily life.
- **Forest bathing (shinrin-yoku)** is promoted for mental health.

This is not anti-modern—this is **wise modernization.**

Disaster Resilience Rooted in Nature

Japan faces frequent natural disasters—earthquakes, tsunamis, and typhoons. But its resilience lies in:

- **Respecting nature's power,** not fighting it
- Building **earthquake-resistant structures** using local materials
- Planting **protective forests** along coastlines
- Practicing **community preparedness** rooted in unity and cooperation

Instead of dominating nature, Japan listens to it—and builds accordingly.

Challenges Still Remain

Of course, Japan faces environmental concerns too:

- Industrial pollution in the past (e.g., Minamata disease)
- High reliance on imported food and fossil fuels
- Urban sprawl in some areas

But what makes Japan different is its **cultural commitment** to change and its **collective responsibility.**

What Can We Learn from Japan?

- **Spiritual traditions can guide modern sustainability**
- **Discipline and community behavior matter more than rules alone**
- **Nature must be a part of life—not just a place to visit**

Japan shows us that **progress and preservation** don't have to be opposites. In fact, they thrive best when they go **hand in hand.**

5.4 Native Tribes & Their Sustainable Living Practices

"They took only what they needed and gave back more than they took."

Long before modern civilizations shaped the world with technology, **indigenous tribes** lived in deep harmony with nature. They didn't see themselves as masters of the Earth—but as **part of it.** Their lifestyles, customs, and spiritual beliefs reflect a powerful truth: **sustainability is not a new idea—it's an ancient way of life.**

Living With, Not Against, Nature

Across continents—from the **Native Americans** to the **Adivasis of India,** from the **Maasai in Africa** to the **Aboriginal Australians**—tribal communities live with profound **ecological wisdom:**

- They **hunt and gather** only what they need
- They **rotate farming areas** to allow soil to recover
- They use **natural materials** without creating waste
- They believe in **sacred groves, forest spirits, and ancestral land.**

To them, Earth is not property—it's a **parent.**

Wisdom in Simplicity

While the modern world chases growth, tribal knowledge values **balance:**

- **Zero-waste living** was practiced long before the term existed
- Medicinal plants were used for healing—without overharvesting
- Rivers, animals, and mountains were treated as **relatives,** not resources

Their traditions show us that **low consumption** doesn't mean **low quality** of life—it means **respectful living.**

Modern Displacement and Struggles

Despite their sustainable ways, native communities often suffer:

- **Forced displacement** due to development projects
- **Loss of land rights and identity**
- **Climate change** affecting their fragile ecosystems
- **Cultural erosion** as younger generations move away

Ironically, the people who did the least to harm the planet are now **the most vulnerable.**

Why Their Knowledge Matters Today

Scientists, environmentalists, and governments are finally realizing what tribal communities knew all along:

- **Traditional ecological knowledge (TEK)** helps manage forests and water bodies

- **Community-based conservation** is more effective than top-down approaches
- Their values of **interdependence** and **gratitude** offer a **moral compass** for sustainability

If we want to build a better future, we must **listen to the past.**

What Can We Learn From Native Tribes?

- **Sustainability is a mindset, not a product.**
- **Culture can be a solution—not a barrier—to environmental action.**
- **Wisdom doesn't always wear suits or speak in numbers—it can live in huts and speak through songs.**

Tribal stories are not just fading tales of the past—they are **blueprints** for a livable future.

Chapter 6: Psychological Impact of Nature Loss on Humans

6.1 Mental Health Crisis & Nature Deficiency

"When we disconnect from nature, we disconnect from ourselves."

As cities grow and forests shrink, a silent crisis is unfolding—not just in the environment, but in the **minds of people**. The rise of anxiety, depression, loneliness, and burnout is now being linked to a surprising but powerful cause: **nature deficiency**.

The Nature-Mind Connection

Human beings evolved in natural environments. For thousands of years, our survival depended on observing skies, reading seasons, and moving through forests and fields. Nature wasn't just a background—it was **home**.

Today, we spend up to **90% of our lives indoors**, surrounded by concrete, screens, and artificial lighting.

This unnatural lifestyle leads to:

- **Sensory overload** in noisy urban environments.
- **Reduced exposure to sunlight** and fresh air.
- **Disrupted circadian rhythms** from screen time.
- **Mental fatigue** due to constant stimulation without rest.

Scientific Evidence

Modern research confirms what our ancestors knew instinctively:

- People who live near **green spaces** report **lower levels of stress.**
- Time in nature improves f**ocus, creativity, and emotional regulation.**
- Children raised with access to parks or gardens have **better cognitive development.**
- Forest walks have been shown to lower **cortisol levels (stress hormone)** significantly.

Nature is not just scenery—it's **therapy**.

Nature Deficiency: The Urban Epidemic

In cities, millions suffer from:

- **Digital addiction**
- **Social isolation** despite being surrounded by people
- **Emotional numbness** and burnout
- **Nature amnesia**—a loss of connection with the seasons, animals, and plants

We're forgetting how to listen to the wind, watch the clouds, and sit with silence.

Reclaiming Our Connection

- The solution doesn't always require grand changes:
- A daily walk in a park
- Having indoor plants or a home garden
- Spending weekends in natural settings
- Mindful moments outdoors—watching birds, touching leaves, listening to rain

These simple acts **recharge the brain, soothe the heart, and awaken the soul.**

What Can We Learn?

- **Mental health is deeply rooted in our environment**
- **Nature is not a luxury—it's a human need**
- **Healing the Earth is also about healing ourselves**

As we restore forests, rivers, and skies, we also begin to restore something within us: **peace**.

6.2 The Rise of Stress and Depression in Concrete Jungles

"The more we build upwards, the more we fall inward."

The modern cityscape, with its towering buildings and endless traffic, symbolizes progress. Yet behind the glossy surface lies a silent epidemic—**rising stress, anxiety, and depression**. The more disconnected we become from nature, the more we struggle within ourselves.

Life in the Urban Labyrinth

In concrete jungles, life moves fast. There's noise, crowds, deadlines, and distractions. While cities offer opportunities and comfort, they often **steal peace and personal space**.

Urban environments are associated with:

- **Higher levels of noise and air pollution.**
- **Increased competition and work pressure.**
- **Reduced access to green spaces**.
- **Overstimulation and lack of silence.**

The mind becomes a battlefield—restless, anxious, and fatigued.

The Psychological Toll

Multiple studies have shown:

- **City dwellers** are more likely to develop **mood disorders** than rural residents.
- Rates of **depression, burnout, and insomnia** are significantly higher in urban settings.
- Urban youth often show signs of **emotional detachment and attention disorders.**

When the **external world never slows down,** the **internal world collapses.**

Missing: A Space to Breathe

In traditional villages or nature-rich environments, people had:

- Open skies and clean air
- Space to walk, talk, and connect
- A slower rhythm of life aligned with nature

In contrast, city life often compresses the human spirit—physically, emotionally, and mentally.

Coping Mechanisms or Escapes?

To handle the pressure, people often turn to:

- **Digital distractions.**
- **Substance abuse or overconsumption.**
- **Mindless entertainment.**
- **Social media validation.**

These are not solutions—they're **escapes from reality.**

The Need for Urban Mindfulness

Even in cities, nature can be reclaimed:

- Creating **urban green zones,** terrace gardens, and vertical forests
- Encouraging **breaks from screens** and digital detoxes
- Building **community spaces** that foster real human connection

Introducing mindfulness and nature-based therapy into daily life

A small patch of green can sometimes do **more for mental health than a hundred motivational quotes.**

What Can We Learn?

- **Progress without peace is not success.**
- **Mental health must be part of urban planning.**
- **Even in a city, we must find our moments of stillness and green.**

The city may be made of concrete, but **the soul still longs for soil.**

6.3 The Healing Power of Green Spaces & Biophilic Design

"Nature doesn't ask for attention—yet it heals the unnoticed wounds."

In a world overwhelmed by concrete, steel, and screens, **green spaces act like gentle medicine**. Parks, trees, rooftop gardens—even a single potted plant—can soothe a tired mind. This isn't a poetic idea; it's a scientifically proven truth.

What Is Biophilic Design?

Biophilia means the **innate human connection with nature.**

Biophilic design is the practice of **integrating natural elements into built environments**—bringing nature in instead of pushing it out.

It includes:

Natural lighting and ventilation

Use of wood, stone, and water features

Indoor plants and green walls

Visual access to nature through windows

Organic shapes and nature-inspired textures

This isn't just architecture—it's **therapy built into space**.

Why Green Spaces Matter

Green spaces offer more than beauty. They:

- **Reduce stress and anxiety**
- **Improve mood and cognitive function**
- **Encourage physical activity and social bonding**
- **Lower blood pressure and strengthen immunity**

Hospitals with gardens see patients recover faster. Schools with greenery show higher focus in children. Offices with plants report less burnout. Nature heals without asking anything in return.

Examples That Inspire

- **Singapore**, known as a "City in a Garden," uses biophilic principles in urban planning.
- **Tokyo**, despite its density, has community parks and green rooftops throughout.
- **Modern workplaces** like Google and Amazon include natural design for employee well-being.
- **Architects worldwide** are now designing homes, hospitals, and schools with nature as the central theme.

The message is clear: **Well-being starts with our surroundings.**

Reconnecting with Nature, Even in Cities

Even without big budgets, we can all start small:

- Keep indoor plants
- Visit local parks regularly
- Grow herbs on balconies or windowsills
- Choose natural materials for home interiors
- Prioritize daylight and fresh air indoors

A single tree can be a place of peace. A flower can remind us of beauty.

What Can We Learn?

- **Design is not just about space—it's about spirit.**
- **Where nature thrives, humans heal.**
- **Cities don't need to suffocate—they can breathe too.**

Biophilic design isn't just the future of architecture—it's the **future of well-being.**

Chapter 7:
Can Technology Save Us?

7.1 AI & Sustainability: A Ray of Hope?

"What if the mind of machines could help save the soul of Earth?"

While human actions have often harmed the planet, human intelligence—and now artificial intelligence—may also offer the solutions we desperately need.

AI (Artificial Intelligence) is no longer just about robots or futuristic fiction. It's being used today to **tackle some of the biggest environmental challenges on Earth.**

Where AI Meets Ecology

AI is being used to:

- Predict climate patterns and extreme weather events.
- Detect illegal deforestation through satellite imagery.
- Optimize renewable energy like solar and wind.

- Monitor endangered species using sound and camera data.
- Improve crop yields through precision farming.
- Track air and water pollution in real time.

These systems analyze massive amounts of data far faster than any human could—helping us make smarter, quicker decisions.

Smart Farming & Forest Protection

- In **India,** AI helps farmers determine the right time to sow seeds, detect pests, and conserve water.
- In the **Amazon,** AI-powered satellites spot illegal logging activity instantly.
- In **Africa,** AI listens to forests—detecting the sound of chainsaws or gunshots, alerting rangers in real time.

Nature can't speak—but AI helps it be heard.

Risks and Responsibilities

- AI is a powerful tool, but it's still a tool—it reflects how we choose to use it.
- If driven by profit alone, AI can increase consumption and deepen inequality.
- If used wisely, it can become a guardian of sustainability.

We must pair technology with ethics, and innovation with intention.

What Can We Learn?

- Technology is not the enemy—disconnection is.
- AI is only as wise as the values we teach it.
- Smart systems must serve a sustainable spirit.

The question isn't "Can AI save us?" It's:

Can we use AI to save what truly matters?

7.2 Green Energy Revolution: The Future or a Myth?

"The sun shines for all, but will we harness it for good?"

As the world grapples with rising temperatures, melting glaciers, and polluted skies, the search for sustainable energy has become more urgent than ever. In this quest, the term **"Green Energy Revolution"** has emerged like a beacon of hope.

But is it truly a revolution—or just another myth wrapped in good marketing?

The Promise of Clean Energy

Green energy refers to sources that are renewable and cause little to no harm to the environment:

- **Solar power:** Harnessing energy from the sun.
- **Wind energy:** Turbines that generate power from moving air.
- **Hydropower:** Using flowing water to create electricity.
- **Geothermal energy:** Capturing Earth's internal heat.
- **Biomass energy:** Converting organic waste into fuel.

These sources promise a future free from fossil fuels and carbon emissions.

Success Stories Around the World

- Germany now produces over 40% of its electricity from renewables.
- Iceland runs almost entirely on hydro and geothermal energy.
- India has become a global leader in solar energy, with massive solar parks lighting up rural villages.

These achievements are not dreams—they're already happening.

Challenges in the Path

However, the green path is not without obstacles:

- **High initial costs** of solar panels and wind turbines.
- **Energy storage issues:** How do we store solar power for cloudy days?
- **Dependence on weather:** No wind, no energy.
- **Land use conflicts:** Large solar farms sometimes replace forests or farmland.

Also, mining for rare-earth materials needed for batteries can harm ecosysems.

Green or Just Greener?

Many so-called **"green"** projects are still tied to corporate profits. Some may reduce emissions but ignore issues like social justice, local displacement, or ecosystem disruption.

The question is not just how clean the energy is—but how **ethically** it is produced and distributed.

What Can We Learn?

- Green energy is not a myth—but it's not magic either.
- True revolution lies in changing both our power source and mindset.
- The future is bright—but only if we make space for sunlight, wind, and wisdom.

The Green Energy Revolution is real. But it needs **people, policies, and purpose**—not just **panels and turbines.**

7.3 Innovations: That Help Humans Reconnect with Nature

"Technology isn't the enemy of nature—it can be its greatest ally."

In a world dominated by screens and skyscrapers, our connection with the natural world is fading. Yet, ironically, it's technology—often blamed for this disconnection—that is now opening new doors to rebuild our bond with nature.

This section explores how thoughtful innovation is guiding humanity back to its roots.

Biophilic Design: Bringing Nature Indoors

Biophilic design blends natural elements into modern architecture:

- Green walls, indoor gardens, and natural lighting.
- Use of wood, stone, and water features in living spaces.
- Workspaces that mimic forest environments.

Studies show that such designs improve mental health, creativity, and productivity.

Nature Apps & Digital Awareness

Mobile apps and digital tools are helping people rediscover nature:

- Plant identification apps like PlantSnap or Seek
- Bird song recognizers to identify local species
- Eco habit trackers encouraging daily green practices

Technology is not pulling us away—it's guiding our gaze back to the trees and skies.

Virtual Nature: Healing in Digital Spaces

For those in concrete cities, virtual reality offers a lifeline:

- VR forests, beaches, and waterfalls can reduce stress
- Digital meditation apps use nature sounds for relaxation
- Schools are using AR and VR to teach ecology in immersive ways

Even a simulated forest can remind us of what we're missing—and why we need to protect it.

Smart Farming & Eco-Tech

Innovations in agriculture promote eco-conscious farming:

- Drones and AI for monitoring crop health without chemicals.
- Soil sensors that prevent over-irrigation.
- Vertical farming to reduce land use and pesticide reliance.

These tools not only feed us—but protect the land that feeds us.

Nature Meets Tech: A New Relationship

The future doesn't have to be humans vs. nature. It can be humans with nature, powered by innovation:

- Eco-tourism platforms preserving ecosystems.
- Blockchain tracking sustainable sourcing.
- AI used to predict poaching or deforestation patterns.

It's not about rejecting progress—but about redirecting it toward balance.

What Can We Learn?

- Technology can **reconnect us,** not just **distract us.**
- Innovation is powerful—but intention gives it direction.
- The best kind of progress is one that respects its roots.

When used wisely, technology can become the bridge between our modern lives and the ancient wisdom of nature.

Chapter 8:
The Role of Education & Spirituality

8.1 Schools & Colleges: Are We Teaching Sustainability?

"We teach children how to count, but do we teach them what truly counts?"

Education is more than information—it's transformation. And in the face of a global environmental crisis, the question arises: **Are our schools and colleges preparing students to protect the planet they will inherit?**

What's Missing in the Curriculum?

While most institutions offer environmental science as a subject, the **depth and urgency** of the ecological crisis are often lost in textbooks and exams.

- Sustainability is treated as a **topic,** not a **mindset.**
- Nature is studied in **theory,** not **experienced.**
- Green practices are **rarely** part of daily school life.

We don't need more data—we need **deep awareness** and an **emotional connection** to nature.

Education That Inspires, Not Just Informs

Some progressive institutions are showing the way:

- Schools with **eco-clubs, tree-planting days,** and **zero-waste campuses**
- College courses combining **ecology with ethics, environmental law, and community service**
- **Outdoor classrooms, nature trails,** and **field visits** becoming regular learning tools

These models show that **learning about nature can happen best in nature.**

The Role of Teachers & Institutions

Teachers can shape a generation's attitude towards the Earth:

- Introducing green habits like **waste segregation, water conservation**
- Encouraging **project-based learning** focused on local environmental issues
- Making **sustainability part of school values**—not just the syllabus

Colleges too can lead by example through:

- **Green infrastructure.**
- **Sustainable food systems.**
- **Research into climate solutions.**

Education = Empowerment

When young minds understand the **value of nature:**

- They **demand** greener policies
- They **innovate** solutions for a better future
- They become **custodians,** not just consumers

True education doesn't just prepare students for jobs—it prepares them for **life on a shared planet.**

A Way Forward: Solutions for Greening Education

1. **Integrate Sustainability Across Subjects**

   Embed climate and ecological literacy into every discipline, from economics to literature.

2. **Nature-Based Learning**

   Include outdoor learning in the regular curriculum—gardening, trekking, biodiversity mapping, and seasonal observations.

3. **Green Campus Initiatives**

   Transform schools and colleges into living laboratories with solar panels, rainwater harvesting, and composting systems.

4. **Student-Led Eco Projects**

   Allow students to lead local environmental campaigns, audits, and awareness drives.

5. **Teacher Training & Support**

   Equip educators with the tools and training to teach sustainability creatively and meaningfully.

6. **Partnerships with Local Communities**

   Involve nearby farms, NGOs, forest departments, and eco-entrepreneurs in the learning Process.

7. **Annual Green Report Cards**

   Measure and reward sustainable practices in schools and colleges through transparent ecometrics.

What Can We Learn?

- Schools are not just **knowledge hubs**—they're **seedbeds of values.**
- Sustainability must be woven into **every subject, every classroom.**
- The earlier we connect children with nature, the **stronger that bond remains.**

Education can be the most powerful climate action—if we let it be.

Call to action

"Let us not wait for the curriculum to change—let us become the curriculum for change."

8.2 Ancient Scriptures & Their Messages on Nature Preservation

"When we see the Divine in all beings, we stop seeing nature as a resource—and start seeing it as a relationship."

Long before climate change became a crisis, ancient wisdom spoke of harmony between humans and nature. The scriptures of India are not just spiritual texts—they are ecological guidebooks.

Nature as Sacred, Not Separate

In ancient Indian thought, nature isn't outside us—it is us.

The **Pancha Bhoota** (Earth, Water, Fire, Air, and Space) are not elements to be exploited but **divine aspects of life.**

- **Vedas** speak of Prithvi (Earth) as a mother—**"Mata Bhumih Putro Aham Prithivyah"** (Earth is my mother, I am her child).
- **Rig Veda's** hymns praise rivers, mountains, rain, and forests.
- **Upanishads** declare the **oneness of all life**—human, animal, plant, and cosmic.

Nature was not just protected—it was **worshipped.**

Scriptures That Preach Sustainability

- **Bhagavad Gita** speaks of yajna (sacred offering), where giving back to nature is a duty, not a favor.
- **Atharva Veda** includes the Bhumi Sukta, a 63-verse hymn dedicated to Earth.
- **Manusmriti** outlines ethical duties to protect water bodies, trees, and animals.

- **Jainism** promotes Ahimsa towards all life—including the smallest insect.
- **Buddhism** teaches compassion (karuna) and interconnectedness of all beings.

These messages aren't symbolic—they're sustainable by design.

Cultural Practices That Embody Ecology

- **Tulasi plant** is worshipped in households—not just for devotion but for its medicinal and air-purifying properties.
- **Cow (Gomata)** is revered as a symbol of nourishment and gentleness.
- **Peepal tree, rivers like Ganga, hills like Govardhan,** and even the **sun and moon** are treated as deities.
- Festivals like **Vanamahotsava, Nag Panchami,** and **Makara Sankranti** have ecological roots.

These traditions embed **reverence for nature into daily life.**

A Message for Modern Times

Ancient wisdom reminds us:

- Nature is not a commodity—it's a **community** we belong to.
- Spirituality without ecology is incomplete.
- If we listen deeply, the scriptures don't just tell us to pray—they tell us to **protect.**

What Can We Learn?

- Sacredness can drive **sustainability** more powerfully than fear.

- The solutions of the future may lie in the **wisdom of the past.**
- Our scriptures don't just preach—they **preserve.**

To revive nature, we must first revive our connection with it.

And perhaps, that begins with reading the Earth like a scripture.

8.3 Meditation & Mindfulness: Reconnecting with Inner and Outer Nature

"If you truly love nature, you will find beauty everywhere—even within."

The journey to heal the planet begins with healing ourselves.

In a fast-paced, noisy world, we have become disconnected not just from nature—but from our own inner stillness. Meditation and mindfulness offer a way back, helping us reconnect with the Earth, one breath at a time.

Inner Calm, Outer Awareness

Meditation is more than stress relief—it's awareness.

Mindfulness teaches us to observe, not consume. To appreciate, not exploit.

When we slow down:

- We notice the **song of a bird,** the **breeze on our skin,** and the **cycle of seasons.**
- We shift from "How can I use nature?" to "How can I live with nature?"

In that silence, compassion grows.

In that stillness, action becomes more intentional.

Ancient Practices, Modern Relevance

- **Buddhist mindfulness** encourages walking meditation in forests—each step with gratitude.
- **Yogic breathing (Pranayama)** connects us with air—reminding us of its sacredness.
- **Dhyan (Meditation)** creates space between impulse and action—reducing overconsumption.
- **Vipassana** teaches observation of nature and the self as one.

When we meditate under a tree, we don't just gain peace—we remember our roots.

The Ecological Impact of Mindful Living

Mindfulness leads to:

- **Conscious consumption**—buying only what we need.
- **Minimalism**—valuing simplicity over excess.
- **Gratitude**—towards water, food, air, and the labor behind it.
- **Reduced waste**—as we become aware of our daily choices.

Environmentalism becomes not a burden—but a **natural extension** of inner clarity.

The Earth Reflects the Mind

- A polluted Earth often reflects a **cluttered mind.**
- A clean, calm environment mirrors **mental balance.**

- Just as we prune a plant, we must prune our thoughts.

If every individual becomes mindful, a society becomes more sustainable.

What Can We Learn?

- Inner awareness leads to outer responsibility
- Meditation isn't escape—it's engagement with presence
- Mindfulness is the seed of a sustainable future

When we care for our inner world, we start caring for the outer one.

A peaceful mind makes a peaceful planet.

Chapter 9:
Practical Steps for Every Individual

9.1 Daily Practices to Restore Human Values

“Change doesn’t begin with policies or protests—it begins with people.”

In the rush for progress, we are slowly losing what truly makes us human: compassion, honesty, humility, and gratitude. These are not just moral ideals—they are essential pillars for a sustainable world. When values erode, so does our connection to each other, to nature, and to purpose.

The good news? Restoring values doesn't require a revolution—it starts with small, conscious daily actions.

Why Human Values Matter

Human values are the foundation of a harmonious society and a healthy planet.

When values like respect, empathy, and responsibility are weakened, the symptoms show up everywhere—climate apathy, greed, social unrest, and environmental exploitation.

To heal the Earth, we must also heal our inner worlds.

Small Habits, Big Impact

A value-based life is built one step at a time. These simple daily practices can bring powerful change:

- **Begin the Day with Awareness**

  Spend 5–10 minutes in silence, prayer, or reflection. Aligns the mind with purpose and Peace.

- **Speak with Kindness**

  Words can uplift or wound. Choose empathy in daily conversations—at home, school, or work.

- **Conscious Consumption**

  Refuse single-use plastic. Reuse what you can. Buy only what you need. Live simply.

- **Serve Without Expecting**

  Help someone without expecting a reward. It could be a smile, a kind word, or helping a stranger.

- **Digital Discipline**

  Limit distractions. Use screens to learn, connect, and grow—not to escape.

- **Reconnect with Nature**

  Walk barefoot on grass, water a plant, notice a tree—small acts, big grounding.

- **End the Day with Reflection**

  Ask yourself: "Did I act with love today?" This builds self-awareness and responsibility.

"Change doesn't always begin on the global stage-it begins in your living room, in your plate, on your daily habits."

Values Are Contagious

When even one person lives mindfully:

- Families become more peaceful
- Workplaces become more ethical
- Children grow up seeing integrity in action

We don't just **teach** values—we **transmit** them by living them.

A Daily Pledge for a Value-Based Life

- I will live with awareness.
- I will treat people, animals, and the planet with respect.
- I will practice kindness and honesty.
- I will grow in gratitude, and act in service.

A Culture of Daily Values

We can create an ecosystem where values flourish. Some ideas:

- **Gratitude Journals**

  Write down 3 things you're thankful for daily. Builds a mindset of abundance and peace.

- **Value Circles**

  Small community or family gatherings to share real-life stories of kindness, honesty, and service.

- **Role Model Recognition**

  Celebrate people—known or unknown—who embody values. Let their stories inspire others.

- **Micro-Challenges**

  7-day kindness challenge, "No plastic", zero-waste week, speak-only-positive challenge. make values fun and actionable.

Values Are the Roots of Sustainability

Just as a tree cannot thrive without deep roots, a society cannot survive without deep values. True sustainability is not just in **what we do, but in who we are.**

And who we are is revealed—one day, one choice, one habit at a time.

"In a world of noise, human values are the quiet revolution. And the best place to begin is within".

9.2 Minimalism & Sustainable Living: A Personal Choice

“We are not rich by what we own—but by what we can live without.”

In a world driven by consumerism, where more is often mistaken for better, minimalism offers a quiet revolution. It invites us to ask: What do I trulsy need? What truly adds value to my life?

Minimalism isn’t about giving up comfort—it’s about giving up clutter. In our homes. In our minds. And on our planet.

The Cost of Excess

Every item we buy—be it a gadget, garment, or grocery—has a hidden cost:

- **Environmental Cost:** Resource extraction, energy use, pollution
- **Emotional Cost:** Stress from maintaining, cleaning, and organizing things
- **Spiritual Cost:** Disconnection from simplicity, peace, and purpose

Our overflowing closets mirror our overwhelmed minds. And the Earth bears the burden.

Minimalism: A Lifestyle, Not a Trend

Minimalism is not deprivation. It is intentional living.

- **Fewer things, deeper joy**

  You own less, but appreciate more.

- **More space, more clarity**

  Physical simplicity brings mental calm.

- **Less waste, more sustainability**

  Every mindful choice reduces your ecological footprint.

Simple Ways to Begin

Start small. Stay consistent. Let your life breathe.

- **The One-In, One-Out Rule**

  For every new item you bring in, let go of one.

- **Buy with Intention**

  Ask—do I really need this?

- **Declutter With Purpose**

  Donate what you don't use. Give it a second life.

- **Buy for Need, Not for Mood**

  Ask: "Will this matter to me in 6 months?"

- **Choose Quality Over Quantity**

  Invest in fewer, longer-lasting essentials.

- **Digital Minimalism**
- Unsubscribe. Turn off notifications. Clear your digital clutter too.

Sustainable Living: Beyond the Buzzword

Sustainability is not just about bamboo toothbrushes or cloth bags—it's about mindful systems:

- **Local and Seasonal Eating**

  Reduces carbon footprint, supports farmers, improves health.

- **Slow Fashion**

  Reuse, repair, and resist fast fashion cycles.

- **Eco-Friendly Homes**

  Use less energy. Harvest rainwater. Compost your waste.

- **Sustainable Celebrations**

  Simple festivals, zero-waste weddings, planet-positive parties, Use cloth bags, metal bottles, bamboo brushes.

The Power of Personal Choice

Every rupee spent is a vote—for or against the planet.

When you choose less, you're not just simplifying life—you're multiplying impact.

- You consume less, pollute less, waste less
- You inspire others without speaking a word
- You show that peace comes not from more, but from enough

Minimalism as a Spiritual Practice

Almost every ancient wisdom—be it Vedic, Buddhist, or Sufi—celebrates simplicity.

Letting go is not loss—it is liberation.

"Live simply so others may simply live."

-Mahatma Gandhi

Minimalism is not about a number of things.

It's about the quality of life.

It's about conscious choices that align with values, not trends.

It's about freedom from what doesn't matter—to focus on what truly does.

Minimalism is not emptiness—it's clarity. It's choosing value over volume.

9.3 Rewilding Cities & Homes: Simple Yet Powerful Actions

"Nature doesn't need us. We need nature. And perhaps, it's time we invited her back."

In the race for urbanization, we've built concrete jungles and forgotten the living ones. But rewilding is not just for forests—it begins at home, on balconies, terraces, sidewalks, and community parks.

Rewilding isn't about going back to the past—it's about bringing nature back into the present.

What is Rewilding?

Rewilding means restoring natural ecosystems in places they once thrived.

- **Urban Rewilding:** Greening cities by adding native plants, reviving water bodies, and creating space for birds, bees, and biodiversity.
- **Home Rewilding:** Bringing nature into your living space—no matter how small.

Rewilding is healing—of land, air, water… and ourselves.

Why Rewilding Matters

- **Mental Health:** Studies show greenery reduces stress, anxiety, and depression.
- **Climate Cooling:** Trees and plants regulate temperature and improve air quality.
- **Biodiversity Boost:** Small green patches become microhabitats for bees, butterflies, birds, and soil organisms.

- **Water Management:** Natural vegetation helps recharge groundwater and prevent floods.

Even a pot on a windowsill is a step toward rebalancing the urban ecosystem.

Simple Actions to Rewild Your Home

You don't need acres. You need intention.

- **Native Plants, Not Exotic Decoratives**

  Choose local species that support local fauna.

- **Balcony Gardens & Vertical Greens**

  Use railings, walls, and terraces to grow herbs, flowers, and climbers.

- **Seed Balls & Guerrilla Gardening**

  Plant seeds in neglected public spaces—parks, sidewalks, road dividers.

- **Compost at Home**

  Turn kitchen waste into black gold for your plants.

- **Install Bird Feeders & Bee Hotels**

  A small bowl of water and grains invites life back into your space.

Rewilding as a Community Act

One tree is a statement. A hundred is a movement.

- **Community Gardening:** Convert empty plots into shared green spaces.
- **School Gardens:** Teach children to grow, not just consume.

- **Urban Forests:** Support Miyawaki method projects in cities.
- **Adopt a Tree Campaigns:** Encourage families to grow together with their saplings.

Collective rewilding transforms not just spaces, but relationships—with each other and with nature.

Policy Can Help—but People Must Lead

- Municipal policies can create green zones, ban tree-cutting, and incentivize rooftop gardens.
- But real change happens when citizens reclaim their role as caretakers—not just consumers—of land.
- Your street. Your school. Your window. They can all become ecosystems again.

Rewilding is a Return

Not to the past—but to balance.

Not to primitivity—but to peace.

"The closer we are to nature, the closer we are to ourselves."

— Inspired by ancient wisdom

What Can We Learn?

Rewilding is a mindset shift—from domination to collaboration.

- We don't need permission to plant life.
- We don't need vast land to create biodiversity.
- We don't need revolutions to begin restoration.

We need pots. Seeds. Soil. Patience.

And a little wildness in our hearts.

Final Reflection of this chapter: The Power of One

Each choice we make is a vote—for the world we want.

- When you say no to plastic, you vote for oceans.
- When you pause before scrolling, you vote for presence.
- When you grow a plant, you vote for life.

You don't need a title or a team to start change.

You just need intention—and action.

The planet doesn't need perfection.

It needs participation.

"The smallest act of kindness towards the earth is a step towards healing the world."

Chapter 10:
The Future: Hope or Despair?

"The future is not something we enter. The future is something we create."

10.1 Can We Reverse the Damage?

"The best time to plant a tree was 20 years ago. The second-best time is now."

For centuries, we have taken more than we gave. Forests fell, rivers dried, species vanished—and we watched, hoping someone else would fix it. But is it too late? Or can we still reverse the damage?

The answer lies not in fear—but in faith and action.

Facing the Facts, Not Fleeing Them

Yes, the numbers are grim.

- Over 1 million species are at risk of extinction.
- Global temperatures are at an all-time high.
- Microplastics are now in our food, water—even our blood.

But here's the truth: **Nature is resilient. And so are we.**

What Reversal Looks Like

Reversal isn't turning back time.

It's turning toward better choices.

- **Reforestation:** Millions of hectares can be revived through native tree planting.
- **Ocean Cleanups:** Grassroots efforts are removing tons of plastic daily.
- **Wildlife Corridors:** Fragmented habitats are being reconnected to allow safe movement.
- **Regenerative Agriculture:** Restoring soil health while feeding people sustainably.
- **Renewable Energy:** Solar and wind are now cheaper than coal in many regions.

These are not just dreams—they are projects already underway.

Stories of Comeback

- **The Ganges Dolphin,** once nearly extinct, is now making a slow return.
- **Costa Rica** reversed its deforestation through strong policies and eco-tourism.
- **The ozone hole** is healing, thanks to global cooperation on phasing out harmful chemicals.

If nature can bounce back, so can we.

The Role of Each of Us

We can't outsource Earth's healing.

Every act matters.

- Saying no to single-use plastic.
- Supporting local farmers and clean energy.
- Planting native trees and protecting the ones that remain.
- Voting for leaders who prioritize the planet.

Change doesn't require perfection. It requires participation.

Hope Is Not Naive—It's Necessary

Hope doesn't mean ignoring the problem.

It means believing in our power to fix it.

We may not be able to undo everything.

But we can slow, stop, and restore more than we think.

What Can We Learn?

- Damage is not destiny.
- Every degraded landscape can be reborn.
- Every choice—what we eat, buy, vote for—can be a seed of restoration.

We can reverse the damage.

But only if we start—now.

10.2 The Power of Collective Human Consciousness

"Never doubt that a small group of thoughtful, committed citizens can change the world. Indeed, it's the only thing that ever has."

The Earth's healing doesn't require a billion perfect people.

It needs a billion awakened minds—conscious, connected, and committed.

This is the true power of collective human consciousness.

What Is Collective Consciousness?

It's more than mass action. It's mass awareness.

When individuals begin to think, feel, and act with a shared purpose—something shifts. Not just around them, but within them.

- A village starts composting—and waste disappears.
- A city switches to cycles—and smog clears.
- A school teaches kindness to animals—and empathy grows.

One ripple becomes a wave.

And waves move mountains.

Moments When Humanity United

History shows us: when enough people care, change becomes inevitable.

- The **Montreal Protocol** united nations to protect the ozone—and it worked.

- The **Earth Hour movement** turned off lights in 190 countries, showing symbolic unity.
- The **Chipko Movement** in India saw women hug trees to save forests—sparking global eco-awareness.
- The **Greta Thunberg** school strike inspired millions of youth to speak up for the planet.

These weren't accidents. They were signs of awakening.

The Science Behind It

Studies in neuroscience and quantum physics suggest that:

- Thoughts have energy.
- Shared emotions amplify action.
- Group intention can influence outcomes—from healing to harmony.

This is not magic. It's mindful alignment.

How We Can Tap Into It

You are part of the collective. You have influence.

- **Be conscious of consumption**—buy less, waste less.
- **Be intentional with words**—they inspire or injure.
- **Meditate and reflect**—a calm mind is a clear mind.
- **Share what you know**—truth spreads when voiced.
- **Join local or global causes**—community builds momentum.

When you raise your awareness, you raise the collective's vibration.

Unity Is a Superpower

We live in the most interconnected era in history.

One post. One conversation. One decision—can shift thousands.

- When hearts align, habits change.
- When habits align, systems evolve.
- When systems evolve, the planet heals.

What Can We Learn?

- Consciousness is contagious.
- We shape the future with our thoughts and choices.
- The power to transform the world already exists—in us.

The question is not if we can unite.

It's when we realize—we already are.

10.3 A Vision for a Harmonious Tomorrow

"The future depends on what we do in the present."

Imagine a world where nature and humanity coexist—not as separate entities, but as one harmonious force.

A world where the air is clean, the oceans are vibrant, and cities buzz with life—not pollution.

A world where the human heart beats in sync with the Earth's pulse, and every action is rooted in respect for life, no matter how small.

This isn't just a dream—it's a possibility.

A New Paradigm: From Exploitation to Stewardship

The old story—one of domination over nature—is fading.

It's being replaced by a new narrative: one of stewardship.

In this story, we are not conquerors, but caretakers.

- Instead of exploiting forests, we nurture them.
- Instead of draining rivers, we revive them.
- Instead of polluting air, we cleanse it.

A harmonious tomorrow is a tomorrow where humans no longer live above nature, but in harmony with it.

How It Will Look

- **Cities of Green:** Imagine cities with more trees than cars, with roofs that absorb pollution and parks that are sanctuaries for all beings.
- **Zero Waste Economy:** Where every product has a life cycle that leaves no trace—what's discarded today is reused tomorrow.
- **Education for the Future:** Where every child is taught the sacredness of nature, where empathy and sustainability are the foundations of their learning.
- **Energy Revolution:** Imagine a world powered by clean, renewable energy—solar, wind, and tidal—leaving no carbon footprints behind.

The Role of Technology in Harmony

While we may feel overwhelmed by the challenges we face, technology can be our ally.

- **Green Tech:** Innovations like vertical farming, eco-friendly architecture, and AI-powered resource management can revolutionize sustainability.
- **Smart Agriculture:** Using sensors and data to minimize water usage and maximize crop yields, reducing the strain on the land.
- **Eco-Friendly Transportation:** Self-driving electric vehicles and high-speed trains could replace pollution-heavy systems, transforming the way we move.

Technology isn't the enemy—it's the key to unlocking a sustainable future.

The Power of Small Actions, Big Changes

Change often starts with the smallest steps.

- A family growing its own food.
- A community converting its waste into compost.
- A neighborhood starting a carpooling system.

These actions may seem small, but together, they create a wave of transformation. They ripple outwards, touching lives, inspiring others, and building momentum toward a larger shift.

A Vision Within Our Reach

We do not need to wait for some distant utopia. The foundation for a harmonious tomorrow exists in our choices today. Every conscious decision you make can contribute to a future we all want to live in.

It starts with awareness, grows with action, and flourishes with unity.

The future is not an inevitable fate—it's a world we co-create, together.

What Can We Learn?

- The future is ours to shape, not something to fear.
- Harmony is not a distant dream—it's a choice we can make now.
- Every step we take towards sustainability brings us closer to a world where both humanity and nature thrive.

The vision is clear: a tomorrow where we all live in balance—with ourselves, with each other, and with the Earth.

Last page of book

Call to Action: Let's Transform the Future Together

You've read the words, absorbed the insights, and now it's time to act.

This book is not just a collection of ideas—it's a guide to changing how we interact with our world, how we restore balance, and how we pass on a better future. Every concept shared, from restoring human values to rewilding cities, has the potential to change lives.

But real transformation happens when knowledge is put into action.

Here's how you can contribute:

1. **Take the First Step in Your Daily Life**

Start small. Start now.

- Practice mindfulness in your everyday actions.
- Integrate sustainability into your routines—whether it's through composting, reducing waste, or choosing eco-friendly alternatives.
- Reconnect with nature—take time to walk outside, breathe in fresh air, and appreciate the beauty around you.

2. Share Knowledge, Spark Change

Pass the message on!

- Share the key ideas and actions from this book with friends, family, and colleagues.
- Inspire others to take steps toward sustainability and better human values.
- Host community discussions or workshops based on the themes of this book.

3. Join or Start Local Initiatives

Engage with your community.

- Volunteer with environmental or social causes that align with the principles outlined here.
- Start community gardening projects, sustainability programs, or environmental awareness campaigns.
- Advocate for policy changes in your local area—support green initiatives, sustainable infrastructure, and climate action.

4. Support Businesses with Purpose

Make your consumer choices count.

- Choose businesses that align with the values of sustainability, fairness, and ecological responsibility.
- Support those who prioritize ethical production, reduce waste, and contribute positively to society and the environment.

5. Reflect and Reimagine the Future

Your perspective matters.

- Reflect on how the ideas presented here can influence your personal and professional life.
- Use the wisdom from these pages to create a vision of a world that values both humanity and the Earth.
- Stay committed to nurturing a harmonious tomorrow, regardless of how small your contribution may seem.

We Need You. The World Needs You.

By adopting the principles of rewilding, sustainability, and human-centered values, you can be part of the solution. Together, we can rebuild a future that balances progress with preservation, development with compassion.

The journey starts with one action. Let it be yours.